TOOTH TALES
from around the World

Marlene Targ Brill • Illustrated by Katya Krenina

Charlesbridge

A tooth is loose! What do you do? You jiggle it and wiggle it. You eat apples. You stand on your head. You string your tooth to a doorknob. You hold contests to see whose tooth twists the most.

Why? You want that tooth to come out.
You want the tooth fairy to come!

But the stubborn tooth hangs on, sometimes by just a thread. Until one day, you take a bite. Something hard rolls from side to side in your mouth, tasting salty from blood. You spit out a sharp lump.

It's your tooth! Now what do you do? Save it? Throw it away? Give it to someone for safekeeping?

For a long, long time, children around the world have followed special customs when they lose their teeth. Today, one popular custom is to leave each tooth for the tooth fairy. This good fairy sneaks into your room while you sleep and takes your tooth. You never hear or see a thing. But in the morning, you discover a surprise under your pillow—maybe a coin, a small present, or a snack sits where the tooth once was.

How does this treat get there? And who is the tooth fairy? No one knows for sure. But beliefs about lost baby teeth go back thousands of years, to a time when stories were passed by word of mouth, a time before anyone ever heard of the tooth fairy.

Almost five thousand years ago, some people in Asia and Africa thought teeth were a sign of strength. They saw that teeth and bones stayed as hard as stones long after a person died.

Ancient Egyptians believed that the sun helped make teeth
even stronger. They threw lost teeth toward the sun saying: GIVE ME
A BETTER
ONE FOR IT.

Over the years, many groups have believed that everyone has a spirit that lives on after people die. Some early Europeans thought that these spirits could live forever as long as their bodies were buried with all of the parts, including the teeth. To save baby teeth, mothers put them in barrels, pockets, or pots. They returned these teeth to their children when they grew up.

Other groups worried that evil spirits might find their children's teeth. They thought these spirits could use the teeth to gain power over the children and hurt them. Both bad spirits and good spirits became known as fairies and witches.

Parents around the world did special things to keep their children's teeth safe from bad witches and fairies. Australian mothers crushed each lost baby tooth into food and ate it. They hoped that a new tooth as strong as iron would last forever in their child's mouth.

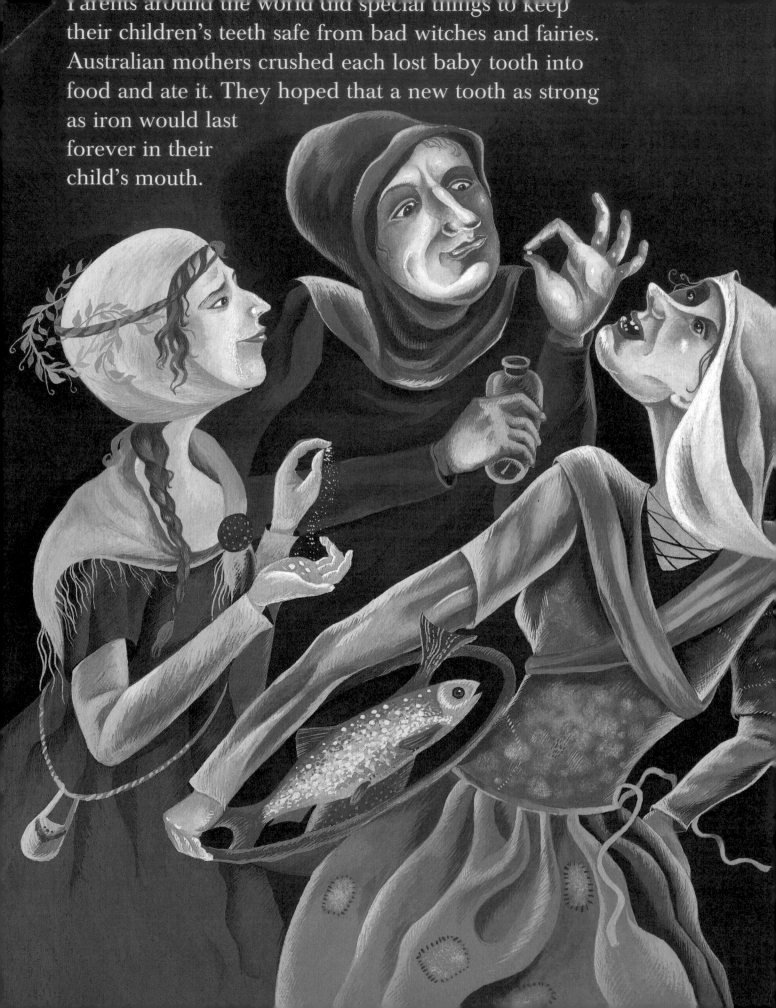

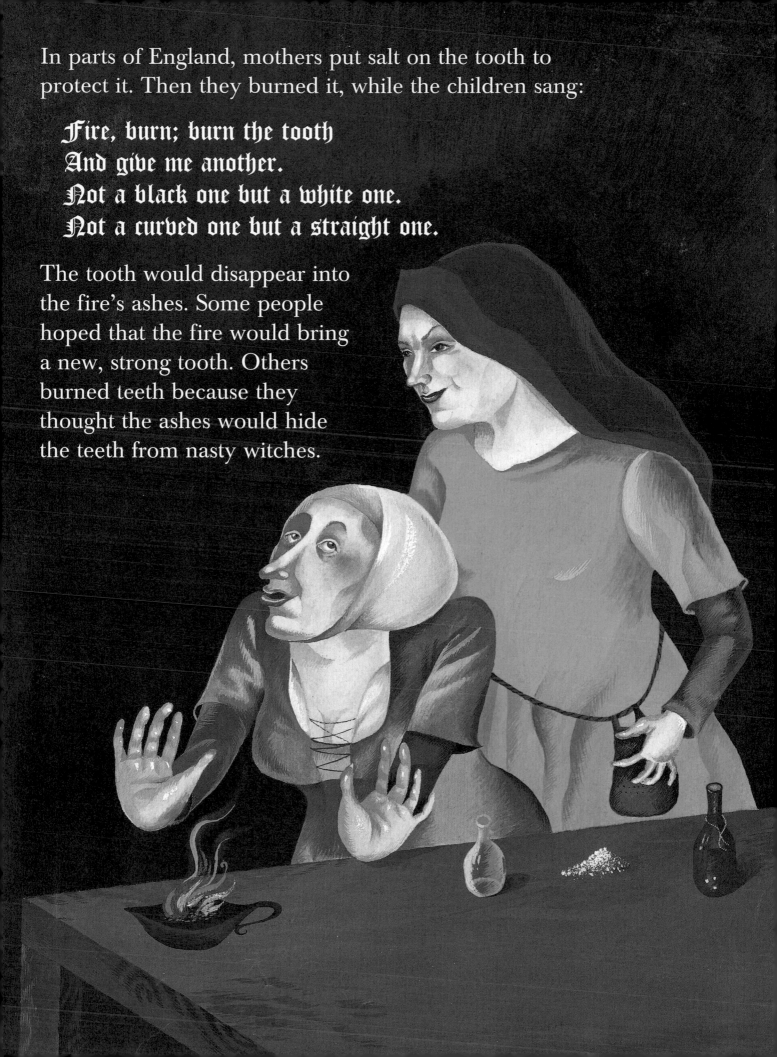

In parts of England, mothers put salt on the tooth to protect it. Then they burned it, while the children sang:

> Fire, burn; burn the tooth
> And give me another.
> Not a black one but a white one.
> Not a curved one but a straight one.

The tooth would disappear into the fire's ashes. Some people hoped that the fire would bring a new, strong tooth. Others burned teeth because they thought the ashes would hide the teeth from nasty witches.

Another way people kept teeth from evil witches was by giving them to animals. Witches were said to dislike certain animals, such as rats and snakes, so people thought teeth would be safe with them. Children hid their teeth near nests, under rocks, or behind fireplaces, anywhere rats and snakes might find them.

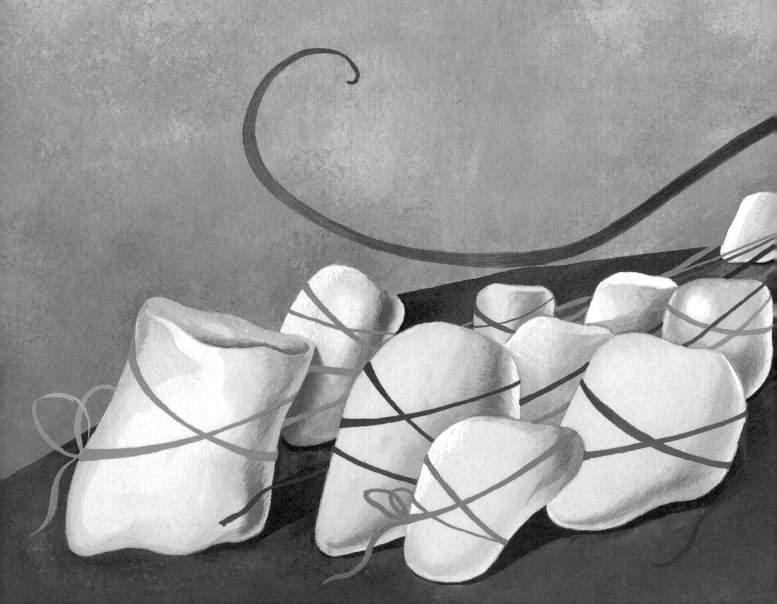

Ilocano children of the Philippines pulled
out their teeth with string. Then they hid the
teeth and the string in rat holes. The string
was to help the rats drag the teeth away.

Over the years, the custom of giving teeth to
animals took on new meaning. Boys and girls
still offered baby teeth to them, but now they
asked sharp-toothed animals—squirrels, cats,
dogs, wolves, even hyenas—to bring them
strong teeth in return.

Cherokee Indian children asked for beaver
teeth. The children ran around their homes
with their teeth. Then they threw the teeth
on the roof, shouting:

Beaver put a new tooth in my jaw!

Beaver put a new tooth in my jaw!

Beaver put a new tooth in my jaw!

Beaver put a new tooth in my jaw!

Other people did not like the idea of any animal finding a child's tooth. Until the late 1800s, parents in Canada and in parts of England and the eastern United States burned their children's teeth or hid them to keep them from animals.

They worried that a tooth just like the animal's would grow where the lost tooth had been. If a pig found their child's tooth, a pig's tooth might grow in its place!

In many cultures, the most popular creature of all was the tooth mouse. Children from Russia, New Guinea, and Egypt thought that mice could live through anything. They knew that mice had teeth that grew healthy and sharp, even after breaking. Some German and Armenian children believed mice were dead relatives who came back to life to help them grow strong teeth.

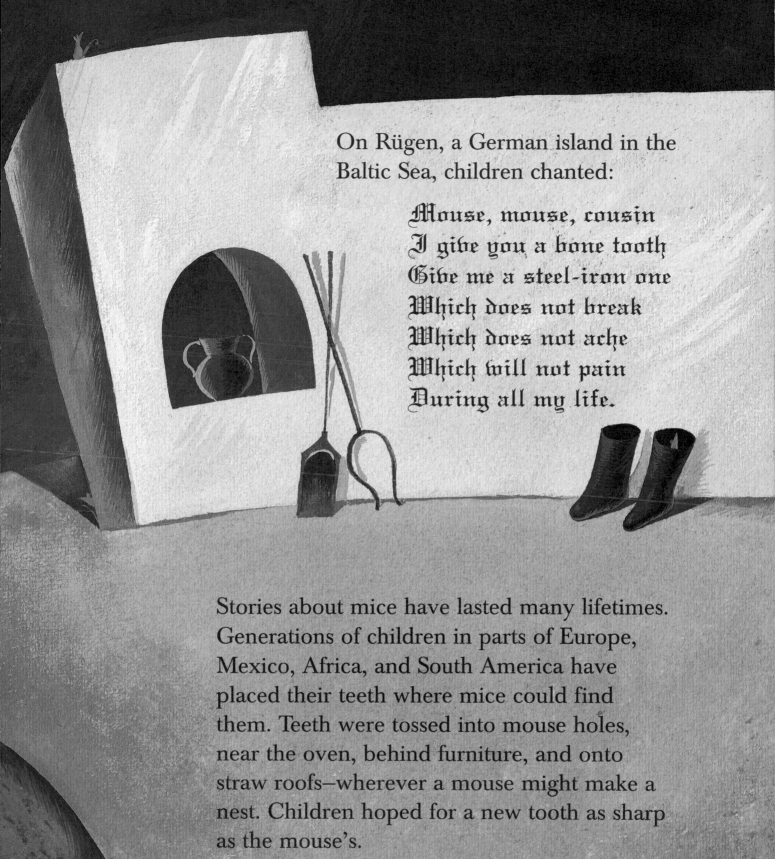

On Rügen, a German island in the
Baltic Sea, children chanted:

Mouse, mouse, cousin
I give you a bone tooth
Give me a steel-iron one
Which does not break
Which does not ache
Which will not pain
During all my life.

Stories about mice have lasted many lifetimes.
Generations of children in parts of Europe,
Mexico, Africa, and South America have
placed their teeth where mice could find
them. Teeth were tossed into mouse holes,
near the oven, behind furniture, and onto
straw roofs—wherever a mouse might make a
nest. Children hoped for a new tooth as sharp
as the mouse's.

It was more than 100 years ago that children in Europe first began to receive treats from the tooth mouse. Sometimes, they found food. Other times, they found a coin or a small present. Everyone liked the idea of getting something in exchange for a lost tooth.

As time passed, a new legend began. People in the United States remembered their parents telling them about a good fairy who took away lost teeth. This fairy became known as the tooth fairy.

Since the 1940s, the belief in one fairy called the tooth fairy has also become popular in parts of Canada, Spain, and Great Britain. Children in families that follow the custom find treats from the tooth fairy whenever a baby tooth falls out. That's up to twenty tooth fairy visits for twenty baby teeth!

These children usually hide their lost tooth in secret places. Most often, they tuck it under a pillow at night. Some boys and girls hide their tooth in a glass of water, inside a slipper, or under the bed.

A few even have tooth pillows to keep their tooth from getting lost in the sheets, or they write letters asking to save the tooth for their collection. For all this work, the tooth fairy usually leaves a coin.

Today, children everywhere continue to follow different customs to mark losing their teeth. In countries such as Mexico and Poland, they still leave baby teeth in hiding places behind ovens and furniture. In return, they find small presents or snacks from the tooth mouse.

There are millions of other boys and girls around the world who have never heard of the tooth mouse. Their mothers have never eaten their teeth or thrown them into fires to keep them safe. They have never heard of evil witches or spirits that steal teeth. But when their teeth come out, these children are glad that they *have* heard of the tooth fairy.

For Fay, Arlene, my editor Kelly, and everyone who believes in the tooth fairy
—M. T. B.

To my dear nieces, Svetochka and Lidochka, who will soon
come to America and meet the tooth fairy
—K. K.

Author's Note

Tooth Tales from around the World presents just a few of the many customs and sayings related to losing baby teeth. These beliefs vary within and among cultures, and there are so many practices that I was unable to include them all.

I found many people helpful as I gathered this information. Special thanks go to Rosemary Wells, Ph.D., retired assistant professor of dental hygiene, Northwestern University Dental School, and curator, The Tooth Fairy Museum, Deerfield, Illinois; William Thomas Jr., M.D., pathologist; Lyn Persson, head children's librarian, Wilmette Library, Wilmette, Illinois; the reference librarians of the American Dental Association; and Nina Jaffe, folklore specialist and author, Bank Street College of Education. I would also like to acknowledge the following sources:

Encyclopaedia of Superstitions by E. and M. A. Radford, The Philosophical Library, 1949. Edited and revised by Christina Hole for Hutchinson of London, 1961.

Ethnodentistry and Dental Folklore by William J. Carter, D.D.S., M.S., et al., Dental Folklore Books of Kansas City, 1987.

Folklore of the Teeth by Leo Kanner, M.D., The Macmillan Company, 1928.

The Lore and Language of Schoolchildren, by Iona and Peter Opie, Oxford University Press, 1959.

"The Tooth Fairy: Perspectives on Money and Magic," a paper presented to the 1989 annual meeting of the American Folklore Society by Tad Tuleja, University of Massachusetts.

Text copyright © 1998 by Marlene Targ Brill
Illustrations copyright © 1998 by Katya Krenina
All rights reserved, including the right of reproduction
in whole or in part in any form.

Published by Charlesbridge Publishing
85 Main Street, Watertown, MA 02172
(617) 926-0329
www.charlesbridge.com

Printed in the United States of America
(hc) 10 9 8 7 6 5 4 3 2 1
(sc) 10 9 8 7 6 5 4 3 2 1

Library of Congress Cataloging-in-Publication Data
Brill, Marlene Targ.
Tooth tales from around the world/Marlene Targ Brill;
illustrated by Katya Krenina.
p.   cm.
Summary: Explores how different cultures have viewed losing
teeth and how the idea of the tooth fairy originated.
ISBN 0-88106-398-3 (reinforced for library use)
ISBN 0-88106-399-1 (softcover)
1. Tooth loss–Folklore. [1. Teeth–Folklore. 2. Tooth Fairy.]
I. Krenina, Katya, ill. II. Title.
GR489.3.B75   1998
398'.353–dc21   97-14275

The illustrations in this book are done in gouache on Fabriano watercolor paper.
The display type and text type were set in Berthold Baskerville, Certificate, Manuscript, Nueva, and Perseus.
Color separations were made by Eastern Rainbow Inc., Derry, New Hampshire.
Printed and bound by Worzalla Publishing Company, Stevens Point, Wisconsin
This book was printed on recycled paper.
Production supervision by Brian G. Walker
Designed by Diane M. Earley